The Adventures of
Alonzo the Chicken

Alonzo and
the Meteorite

Written by Debbie Kelly
Illustrated by Monika Filipina Trzpil

This book is dedicated to my nephew William,
who inspired me to create Alonzo.

This book is designed to be dyslexia friendly.
For more information please visit www.bdadyslexia.org.uk

First published in paperback in Great Britain by Digital Leaf in 2013

ISBN: 978-1-909428-27-0

Book printed in the EU.

Contents

Allow me to introduce Alonzo.

He is a chicken and, as chickens go,
he's quite cool. He loves his hat,
his music and having fun. He also has
some very special gadgets and knows
a little bit of magic. And because of this,
Alonzo always has adventures...

Chapter 1

Bump in the Night

It is the beginning of a beautiful day with the sun slowly rising above the treetops. Alonzo is fast asleep in his comfy bed when, suddenly, he finds himself on the floor.

'Oh my goodness! What happened there? Why am I on the floor?' he says.

Alonzo looks around his bedroom and sees that lots of his possessions that were on shelves are now all over the floor. In fact, he realises that everything is out of place.

This is very odd, he thinks, as he starts picking things up and putting them back where they belong.

Alonzo goes downstairs and puts on the television.

'Breaking news,' says the news presenter. 'A meteorite which has been travelling through space has entered the Earth's atmosphere and clipped the planet. At the moment we do not know what, if any, effects this will have. If you notice anything strange, then please call the Meteorite Incident Helpline. The number is coming up on your screen now.'

Gosh, thinks Alonzo. I wonder what will happen next. He decides to go out for a walk to see if anything looks or sounds different.

He sets off down the street, passing houses and shops. Nothing looks different at all. He hears a cat miaow behind him so he turns round to stroke it - but to his surprise he sees a dog! Alonzo feels very confused. He must be hearing things.

As he continues down the road, the dog runs ahead of him, turns round, wags his tail, opens his mouth and miaows! Alonzo is amazed and a little scared. He decides to go and visit his best friend, William the Wise Owl, to see what he thinks of the situation.

4

Chapter 2

Whatever Next?

As Alonzo makes his way to William the Wise Owl's house, he realises there is something very strange going on. The sky has turned yellow and the sun is blue!

This is getting more and more peculiar, thinks Alonzo. Luckily William the Wise Owl isn't called Wise for nothing. Surely he'll understand what is going on.

Finally, Alonzo arrives at William's house and rings the doorbell, which, bizarrely, makes a knocking sound.

William opens the door and drags Alonzo inside. 'Tell me. Am I going mad or are there strange things happening?' asks William.

Alonzo walks across to look out of the window. 'Nope, you're not going mad.

5

It is all very odd. I heard a dog miaow this morning. The sun has turned blue and the sky is yellow. And now the grass has turned black and white and the cows are green! I think it's about time we ring the helpline and report what we've seen.'

While Alonzo starts dialling, William switches on the television.

'Meteorite update,' the news presenter says. 'Unfortunately, the situation is worse than originally thought. It would appear that the meteorite hit our planet so hard that we are now spinning in the wrong direction! That's why things are now the wrong way round. You will have seen that the sky has changed colour and is now yellow, whilst the sun is now blue. This is just one of the many things we are experiencing. Tune in tomorrow for an update from the Prime Minister.'

6

'Oh my goodness me!' says William. 'What do you think of all that, Alonzo?'

As he puts the phone down, Alonzo looks at his friend and sighs. 'I really don't know, not yet. I'm hoping that I can help to come up with a cunning plan.'

'I really hope that, between you and the Prime Minister, you can work something out.'

'Well, William, what about you? You're called William the Wise Owl! Surely you can help come up with an answer.'

'I'm afraid this is beyond me. I have no idea what to do. What if things get worse?'

'William, you are turning into William the Worry Owl! Let's get together tomorrow and put our thinking caps on. We'll see if we can come up with a plan.

With your clever brain and my magic skills, I'm sure we can think of something.'

'You're absolutely right. I'm getting my feathers in a twist for nothing. I'll see you in the morning.'

Chapter 3

Blown Away

The next morning, Alonzo turns on the television to watch the news, and it looks like things have got decidedly worse. In Africa, the zebras have got spots instead of stripes, and the giraffes have got short necks! In the North Pole, the polar bears have changed colour and are now black! What a mess. Alonzo gets ready to visit William and see if he has had any ideas.

It's a nice day, so Alonzo decides to walk across the fields. As he does so, he notices all the things that are the wrong way round, and there are lots of them. He crosses into the next field and the wind suddenly picks up, making it really difficult to make any progress. In fact, the wind is SO strong and blustery that it pushes Alonzo backwards!

9

Eventually, Alonzo arrives at William's house and knocks on the door, which makes a ringing noise. William throws open the door and pulls Alonzo inside. 'Quick, get in. The Prime Minister is about to appear on television to tell us what's going on.'

Alonzo and William settle down on the sofa and wait for the press conference to start.

'And now here is Dave Chaddlesworth, our Prime Minister.'

'Good morning. I am here to give you an update on the meteorite situation. Yesterday a large meteorite clipped our planet, and as a result the Earth is now spinning in the opposite direction. You will no doubt have seen and heard things that are the wrong way round. My top

scientists are working around the clock to work out how to get the world to spin the right way again. I will speak to you again soon but, in the meantime, please do not worry. Everything will be fine. Thank you.'

William gets up from the sofa and turns off the television. 'What do you think of that?'

'I think I may have a cunning plan,' replies Alonzo. 'Let's have some lemonade and I'll tell you all about it.'

Chapter 4

An Idea is Hatched

Alonzo and William grab their drinks and sit back down. 'Come on, then. Tell me your idea. I'm very excited.'

Alonzo takes a deep breath and starts talking. 'So, all we have to do is get the world to spin the right way again to change things back.'

'Well, we kind of know that,' snaps William, 'but how? What are you going to do? Conjure up another meteorite to hit us again? I know you can do magic, Alonzo, but I don't think even you can do that on your own. Even if you could, it might all go horribly wrong. The new meteorite might break up into little pieces, or even worse, knock us into another universe!'

'William, you need to stop panicking and listen. You are absolutely right, another meteorite could spell disaster. But what do you think of this idea? How about if we get all the birds in the world to fly around the planet in the opposite direction to the way it is currently spinning? I think the force from the beating of their wings might be strong enough to stop the Earth from turning, and then push it to spin the right way.'

William looks at Alonzo in stunned silence. 'That is the most ridiculous thing I have ever heard. But do you know what? I think it'll work! What do we need to do next?'

'Well,' says Alonzo, 'we need to speak with the Prime Minister first and tell him our plan. Second, I need to get in contact

with some of our friends on the seven different continents to help spread the word. Then we need to...'

'Alonzo, before you carry on, what about the birds that can't fly? This is a fairly spectacular event and every bird will want to take part and help. How can we get them involved?'

'That is a very good point, William, and you are absolutely right. What about if I cast a special spell for all those birds like penguins, kiwis and emus, so that, on the right day, at the right time, they have the ability to fly with us.'

'That's a great idea, Alonzo. They will be pleased. We really will need the help of everybody.'

'I'm going to go home now and ring the incident line and ask them to put me

15

in touch with the Prime Minister's top scientists so I can put the idea to them. I'll come back in the morning and let you know how I get on.'

'Good luck, Alonzo. I think this is a very good plan. I'll see you tomorrow.'

16

Chapter 5

From Chuckles to Cheers

Once Alonzo gets home, he rings the incident number and explains his plan. As he finishes, there is a deathly silence. Suddenly, the lady on the other end bursts out laughing! 'Are you for real? That is the funniest thing I have heard. I've taken some strange phone calls today, but that one really takes the biscuit!'

Alonzo feels a little put out by her reaction, but believes his plan has real potential. 'Will you please pass my idea on?' he asks, feeling a bit worried that by the time she stops laughing, she will have forgotten.

'Yes, yes. I'll tell someone,' she says through her giggles. 'Don't worry. Thank you for brightening up my day. Goodbye!'

Hmmm. That didn't quite go as expected. However, undiscouraged, Alonzo picks up his address book and looks through it to work out which of his bird friends he needs to contact. Alonzo needs one bird per continent to help co-ordinate the plan and spread the word. Now, let's start with Europe. Who is the best bird to ask? he thinks. As he flicks through the book he spots the name he knows he can trust. Sara the Swan. She's exactly the right bird for the job. Graceful, calm and elegant. As he makes a note of her number, he thinks about who to contact next for Asia.

Alonzo continues looking through his address book until he starts to yawn. He looks at his watch and sees it's nearly midnight! He has been so busy working on the plan that time has completely run away with him. He goes into his bedroom, snuggles down in his bed and immediately falls asleep. It's hard work trying to save the world.

The next morning, Alonzo is woken up by the loud ringing of his phone. As he answers in a sleepy voice, he hears a voice saying, 'Please hold, Mr Alonzo. I'm just connecting you to the Prime Minister, Dave Chaddlesworth.'

Wow! Thinks Alonzo. I need to wake up and clear my head!

'Good morning, Mr Alonzo,' a deep, booming voice says over the phone. 'I have been told that you have come up with an idea which may sort out this back-to-front problem that we have. Please tell me exactly what you plan to do.'

19

Alonzo quickly gathers his thoughts and explains his idea. As he finishes there is a long silence. 'Genius! Pure genius! When will this happen?' asks the Prime Minister.

'Today is Friday and it will take me a few days to get everything organised, so let's say Monday the 16th June at 12 noon. Also, Prime Minister, I could do with your help. I need every single bird to be available for this plan so could you do another public address on television to ask all owners of pet birds to open the doors of their cages for this one evening only, so they can be involved? I will ensure all pet birds return to their rightful owners by the following morning.'

'No problem at all. What about Saturday evening? I will also make sure an advert is placed in the Sunday

21

newspapers, which will give everybody an opportunity to see the message. Is there anything else I can help you with?'

'No, I don't think so, thank you, sir, but I'll keep you updated on how the plan is going.'

'I'll leave you to it then, Mr Alonzo. It sounds like you have everything under control. My secretary will give you my direct number for when we need to talk again. Goodbye.'

'Goodbye, Mr Prime Minister.'

Alonzo sits back on his chair and thinks about the phone call. I'd better get a move on. Lots to organise, birds to talk to and magic to perform.

He starts to make a list.

Chapter 6

Roller Skating Owl

Alonzo sets off to William's house with his list of things to do tucked under his wing.

Busy thinking about his plans and not really paying attention to where he's going, Alonzo suddenly bumps into Dr Darren Duck.

'Oops! Sorry about that, Dr Darren. Didn't see you there. Where are you off to with your medical bag?'

Surprisingly, Dr Darren looks a little sheepish and says in a small voice, 'Hi, Alonzo. It's not where I'm going. It's where I've been.'

'What do you mean?'

'Well, I'm not meant to say anything to you. He wants to explain what happened himself.'

23

'Who does?' asks Alonzo.

'William the Wise Owl.'

'What?!' yelps Alonzo as he starts running across the field as fast as his legs will go.

'Don't be too hard on him,' calls Dr Darren, but Alonzo is out of earshot and doesn't hear him.

When he arrives at William's house, he is completely out of breath and hammers on the door. Eventually, William opens it and stands there waiting for Alonzo to say something, for William has his wing in a sling!

'Just tell me. What did you do?' asks Alonzo.

'Come inside and we'll talk, but please don't be cross.'

Alonzo steps inside and sits down with William. 'Please tell me that you're OK. Well, apart from your wing,' says Alonzo.

'I'm better now I've seen Dr Darren. He's given me some medicine that helps with the pain.'

'So, what happened?'

'It was a silly idea really, and it just all went horribly wrong. I was doing a bit of spring cleaning and sorting out the cupboards, when I discovered a pair of roller skates that I had been given when I was little. I remembered how much fun it was, zooming around on them, so I decided to have a go, and I'm not so good at it now,' he says in a forlorn little voice.

Alonzo starts to smile. 'Oh, William, you funny thing. I am sorry that you have hurt yourself, but I can't believe you

26

thought you'd be able to roller skate like you did when you were little. Sometimes you really aren't a wise owl at all.'

Now William is smiling as well, and they dissolve into fits of laughter. After several minutes they calm themselves down. 'It really is a funny image to think about,' says Alonzo, 'but we need to get on with some serious stuff. The plan.'

Alonzo tells William about his phone call with the Prime Minister and then goes through the list of things that need to be done. 'There are seven phone calls we need to make to our key birds on the different continents. Please can you call Richard the Rainbow Lorikeet in Australasia, Keith the Keel-Billed Toucan in South America, Emily the Eared Grebe in North America and finally, Viv the Vulture in Africa.'

'Wow, that's a lot of phone calls,' says William. 'And I need to tell them the plan, and confirm the date.'

'Yep, that's exactly right. I will be ringing Sara the Swan, who will cover Europe, Francesca the Fairy Bluebird in Asia, and Cara the Chinstrap Penguin in Antarctica. I also need to update the Prime Minister to let him know how we're doing. Once we have completed our calls, I'll make us some tea, and then I'll stay tonight to look after you and keep you company.'

'Oh, Alonzo, that is really kind. Thank you, that'll be nice.'

Chapter 7

Breakfast-Time Blues

The next morning, Alonzo gets up and starts setting the table for breakfast. He lays out the bowls and spoons for their cereal, when William wanders in with a gloomy look on his face. 'What's wrong? You look ever so sad. Did you not sleep very well?'

'Alonzo, I know it's really silly, and I've only just realised, but I'm not going to be able to take part in the plan. I can't fly!'

Alonzo looks at his best friend and sees the big, fat tears sliding down his feathered face. 'Oh, William, please don't cry. I know you're disappointed that you can't fly with your broken wing, but remember you're doing such a great job, helping me with all the phone calls.

You ARE part of this plan. I couldn't do this without you.'

'I know, but it's just... Can't you use some magic to fix my wing?'

'My magic is only for short-term problems. It can't be used to change or fix things longer term. Let's concentrate on the final few phone calls and then talk. Try to have some breakfast and then phone Keith in South America.'

'OK,' says William as he pours himself a bowl of Tasty Tweet Wheats cereal. He then picks up the phone and walks into the next room to make his call.

Alonzo claps a wing to his head. 'Oh, William. How can you possibly take part with a broken wing? I really don't want you to miss out now! You've been part of this plan since the start!'

30

As Alonzo pours himself some cereal, he suddenly grins. He has come up with a fantastic idea! When William comes back into the room, Alonzo grabs his hat and rushes to the front door. 'See you in a bit. Got something really important to do.'

'What?' asks a bemused William.

'See ya!' yells Alonzo as he runs out of the door and across the fields.

Alonzo knows exactly where he needs to go and who he's looking for - Blaze the Buzzard. The only problem is, sometimes he's quite hard to find!

Chapter 8

Finding Blaze

Alonzo sets off to the forest to find Blaze. On his way, he sees Nicola the Nightingale trying to hide in the trees.

'Hello, Nicola! I haven't seen you for ages. How are you?'

'Alonzo! Just look around. Things are the wrong way round. I am very confused.'

'I know, Nicola. A meteorite hit the planet and now it's spinning the wrong way so things are topsy-turvy. It's a nightmare. Have you heard from Sara the Swan about my big plan to sort this out?'

'No. I haven't spoken to her in ages!'

'OK, well, you will. I can't fill you in now because I need to find Blaze the Buzzard, but let's just say that you need to keep next Monday free.'

33

'Ooohh. That sounds intriguing. Can't wait to hear from her. You say you're looking for Blaze. I saw him at the next clump of trees, hunting for food.'

'Thanks, Nicola. I better go and find him. I need his help. See you soon.'

'Bye!'

Alonzo continues into the forest and he comes across a clearing where Blaze is soaring high above the treetops.

Now, how am I going to attract his attention? Alonzo wonders.

Just as he's thinking that, Blaze swoops down into the long grass.

'Blaze! Blaze!' yells Alonzo as he runs towards him. 'I need to talk to you!'

Blaze looks up and starts to walk across the clearing. 'My goodness me. If it isn't

Alonzo the Chicken. I haven't seen you in a very long time.'

'I know,' says Alonzo, 'it's been ages! How are you?'

'Well, apart from these very strange happenings with things being the wrong way round, I'm fine. What can I do for you?'

'Can we go somewhere to talk, please? I really need your help."

As they walk back, Alonzo starts to talk. He tells Blaze all about the meteorite and his plan to help poor old William.

'Do you think you could do it?' asks Alonzo.

'It would be my pleasure. This is exactly what friends are for. Let's go straight back to his house and tell him.

I bet we can change those sad tears into happy ones.'

'Thank you, Blaze. I know this will mean a lot to him and it'll be so much fun as well.'

Chapter 9

Flying High

Alonzo and Blaze decide to show William their plan which, they are sure, will make him smile. They walk through the forest until they find a fallen branch which Alonzo scrambles up. Blaze crouches beside it and Alonzo clambers onto his back. Blaze stretches his wings and within seconds they are soaring across the sky.

'Hold tight! I love riding the thermals!' Blaze cries.

'OK,' replies Alonzo, who is feeling a little queasy. He's not used to flying and Blaze seems to be swooping and swerving all over the place!

Eventually, after what feels like forever, they arrive at William's house.

37

Still sitting on Blaze's back, Alonzo manages to tap on the door and, after a short wait, William opens it.

'Surprise!' shouts Blaze and Alonzo.

'What are you doing?' asks William in a small voice.

'Watch this!' cries Alonzo as Blaze takes off and flies around the field. As they land back at William's front door they see he has a very confused look on his face.

'I don't understand what you are doing,' he says.

'Look at Blaze. He's a big, strong bird. When it's time for the plan, you're going to sit on his back and flap your good wing. This morning you were so upset when you thought you couldn't take part in the plan and now you can!'

William stares at Alonzo and Blaze with

a look of complete and utter delight, and his face breaks into the biggest smile.

'You two are the best friends an owl could possibly have!' he says as tears of happiness slide down his face. 'That is just an awesome idea! Can I have a go now?'

'Of course you can,' replies Blaze. 'Hop on and let's ride that breeze.'

As Blaze flies off, all Alonzo can hear is William hooting with delight.

Chapter 10

Confused Cara

Alonzo goes inside William's house, makes himself a drink and waits for the two of them to return. He pulls out the list of things still to do when suddenly the phone rings. As he answers, he hears a chatter of noise from the other end.

'Calm down! I'll ask him. Yes, yes, I'm sure he'll come up with something...'

'Hello,' says Alonzo. 'Can I help you?'

'Oh, yes. Hi, Alonzo, it's Cara from Antarctica.'

'Hi, Cara. Everything OK?'

'Well, sort of. I've managed to spread the word about the plan. However, some of us non-flying birds are a little worried about flying. We've never done it before and feel the need to learn how to, and

for some practice. Also, I'm a bit confused about what time we should be flying. Is it 12 noon my time, or 12 noon your time?'

'Golly. What a lot to think about. Well, we need every bird to fly at the same time to get the maximum effect, so it'll be 12 noon my time. I'll work out what time that is on the different continents.'

'What about the birds who can't fly? And that includes you, Alonzo.'

'Do you know, I've been so wrapped up in the plan, I hadn't even thought about me flying. You're right. How about I cast a spell for the non-flying birds to be able to practise at night-time only, between now and the plan? Do you think that would work? That gives us one or two nights, depending upon the time zone you're in. Thinking about it, I'll need quite a lot of practice too.'

'That sounds great and should reassure the birds. Also, we don't want to bamboozle the poor humans even more by letting them see us fly. They're already very confused! I'll wait to hear from you about the whole time thing as well, once you've worked it out. Thanks, Alonzo.'

'That's alright, Cara. Leave it with me. I'll cast the flying spell for practising shortly. I just need to let the other birds know so they can have a go too.'

'OK. I'll let you get on as you must be really busy. Speak soon, Alonzo. Bye.'

'Goodbye, Cara.'

Alonzo puts down the phone and sighs. Goodness me, he thinks. That's even more to do!

He picks up his list and starts adding all the other things that need to get done.

When Alonzo finishes the list he hears the gleeful hooting of William.

Excellent, he thinks. I can ask Blaze and William to help me work out the time differences. I need to speak with Prime Minister Chaddlesworth and update him, especially with this latest development about all the non-flying birds.

Blaze and William burst through the front door, full of excitement from their flying trip.

'That was so cool! Better than flying myself!'

Alonzo looks at William, who has the biggest smile on his face. 'I'm thrilled for you, William, I really am. Now I don't want to bring you back to Earth with a bump, but I need some help with the plan.'

44

'Oh, OK. Can Blaze help as well?'

'That would be great. Something has come up that I hadn't thought about.'

'Really? I thought we had everything covered.'

'So did I, but I've had a call from Cara the Chinstrap Penguin. She and the other penguins are really worried about flying. They've never done it before and they want to practise.'

'Oh my goodness! Of course. Why didn't we think of that?'

'Also, she wants to check what time to fly as she's confused. All the birds needs to fly at the same time, so we'll fly at 12 noon our time, which I know will be different all over the world. So we need to work out the time differences for all the different countries.'

45

'Not a problem. We'll start now.'

'Great,' says Alonzo. 'Thank you. I'm going to ring the Prime Minister.'

Chapter 11

Final Details

Alonzo leaves William and Blaze to work out the time differences, and dials the Prime Minister's number.

'Hello,' says a booming voice, 'Dave Chaddlesworth speaking.'

'Oh, hello, Prime Minister. It's Alonzo here.'

'Ah, Alonzo! How's the plan going?'

'Well, that's why I'm ringing. I just want to check that everything is in place for the television address tonight, and the newspaper articles tomorrow.'

'All sorted. Don't worry.'

'That's great, thank you. I've been wondering about how the plan is going to work. We don't want to confuse the human population too much.'

'Mmm. Yes. They are already confused and I'm not sure they can take much more.'

'Exactly,' replies Alonzo. 'I think you need to tell everybody what the plan is. You don't necessarily have to tell them how the non-flying birds are going to fly, just that they are.'

'Are you sure?' asks the Prime Minister. 'Won't this worry people even more?'

'In all honesty, things are already the wrong way round, so I don't think this will surprise them.'

'Good idea. I like your thinking.'

'The other thing, Mr Prime Minister...'

'Please call me Dave,' he interrupts.

'Oh, OK, Dave,' says Alonzo. 'The other thing is that all the non-flying birds are a little worried. I will be casting a spell on

the day itself to give them the ability to fly but they need to practise beforehand, and that includes me! So if I cast a spell now this will give us one or two nights to work out how to use our wings.'

'Golly. I hadn't thought about that. Well, it sounds like everything is coming together. Good luck.'

'Ah, just one more thing. I was thinking about when we are all flying around the world. We will need to know when the world is spinning the right way again, and we won't be able to see...but you will.'

'Mmm. Another very good point. I suppose it may take you quite a while to cause enough force to change the Earth's rotation. So, how can we let you know?'

'Well, the only way I can think of is if we both have a headset with a

49

microphone. We could easily talk that way.'

'Excellent! I'll have a chat with the Secret Service and get one delivered to you. We can check it works on Monday morning.'

'Thanks, Dave. That sounds great. I better go now as I have quite a lot to do. Thanks again. Goodbye.'

'Bye, Alonzo.'

As he puts down the phone, William and Blaze come into the room with reams of paper.

'Goodness me. What is all that?'

'Well, Alonzo,' says Blaze. 'It was more complicated than we thought. There are 24 different time zones; some of them are ahead of our time, some of them behind. It's been a nightmare to work out!'

'Blaze is over-reacting,' says William.

'Yes, it's been difficult, but we've made all our phone calls to our key birds, and got it sorted. Basically, you need to cast your spell for Australasia now, as New Zealand is already 12 hours ahead of us here in the UK. I've spoken with Richard and they are all ready and waiting.'

'Good work, you guys. Thank you. I better cast the flying spell now.' Alonzo wanders into the next room, muttering some magic words under his breath.

Chapter 12

Practice Makes Perfect

The next day, Blaze and William receive several phone calls from all around the world. Things aren't looking too good for the non-flying birds; they really are struggling to get the hang of it. It is much more difficult than they first thought.

There have been reports of birds flying into the sides of icebergs, careering into trees and flying into each other! Today is Sunday and the plan is happening tomorrow!

'What are we going to do?' asks William. 'And where is Alonzo when we need him?'

'He's out practising as he's a bit worried about flying as well,' replies Blaze.

Suddenly there is a thump at the front door. 'What on earth is that?' asks Blaze.

William walks across the room and slowly opens the door. Alonzo is slumped in a crumpled heap with his hat all askew and his sunglasses hanging off his beak.

'Goodness me! Are you OK?'

Alonzo looks up at his friend. 'I've been better. I am not very good at this flying malarkey. It's just so difficult.'

William helps his friend up and into the front room, where Alonzo falls onto a chair. 'How do you do it?' he asks. 'Every time I think I'm doing well, and know what I'm doing, it all goes horribly wrong!'

'My advice,' says Blaze, 'is not to think about it. Just believe that you can, relax and let your wings take over.'

'Do you think that'll help?'

'Absolutely,' replies Blaze. 'I never think about how I fly, I just know that I can.'

'OK. Thank you. I've hurt my beak from flying into the front door, and it feels a bit bruised. I'm going have a bit of a rest, and then have another go.'

'I think that is a very good idea. We'll make sure everything for the plan is going OK and give you an update once you have slept.'

As Alonzo sleeps off his worries, the phone doesn't stop ringing. William and Blaze are having to constantly reassure all the worried birds by giving them the same advice that Blaze gave to Alonzo.

'Yes, yes, I know it's horrible, and you must be getting quite sore from flying into trees all the time, but you will get it. Stop thinking about what you need to do, believe that the magic will work and that you can do it, and then you will be able to,'

explains Blaze to Ollie the Ostrich.

'I know, I know, it must be frustrating, but just think how you will feel when you take part in the plan. The humans don't know how to fix this topsy-turvy problem and they are all depending on us!'

After a few minutes, Blaze says goodbye to Ollie and puts the phone down.

'Goodness me,' says William. 'I didn't expect this to cause so much trouble. I just hope they listen to your wise words and this all works out.'

'I'm sure it will. We just need to believe that the plan will all come together at the right time.'

'Of course it will,' says Alonzo, who has walked up behind them. 'They have all of today and some of tomorrow to build up their confidence. Right, I'm off out again.

I WILL fly! Blaze, fancy coming with me?'

'Love to. Let's go and stretch our wings and soar!'

Chapter 13

The Big Day

The following morning, after a good night's sleep, Alonzo wakes up early and bounds out of bed. Today is Monday, the day of the plan and it's his final chance for some last minute flying practice. His attempt yesterday with Blaze went really well.

He was absolutely right. I just needed to believe in myself and relax, he thought. I wonder how everybody else has been getting on.

Whilst he's getting ready, there's a knock at the door. It's a man from the Secret Service with a parcel.

'Parcel for Mr Alonzo.'

'That's me!'

'May I come in, please? I have a special

delivery for you from the Prime Minister.'

'Is this the headset and microphone?'

'It is indeed. I just need to set it up for you and then we can test it out.'

'How exciting!' says Alonzo.

They both sit down and start putting the equipment together, whilst the Secret Service man explains to Alonzo how it all works.

'We just need to tune this into the same frequency as the Prime Minister's, and then we're all set up. There we are. Now, put this on and talk normally into the microphone. You should be able to hear Prime Minister Chaddlesworth talking to you.'

As Alonzo puts the headset on, he hears Dave's booming voice in his ear. 'HELLO, ALONZO!'

Alonzo nearly jumps out of his feathers! The Prime Minister is so loud in his ear!

'Oh, hello there, Dave. Could you possibly talk a little quieter, please? I only have little ears and you are very loud.'

'Oops, sorry about that, Alonzo. Just wanted to make sure you could hear me.'

'Yes, yes, I can. No worries.'

'Brilliant. So, are we all set for lunchtime? Everything organised?'

'I think so. I'm just off to see William and Blaze, who have been co-ordinating the last few bits and then it's full steam ahead.'

'Fabulous! I thought I'd make one last appearance on television, reminding all the bird owners to open their cages, and then it's all down to you.'

'That's great. Thanks, Dave.'

61

'I really hope this works, Alonzo,' says the Prime Minister in a quiet voice. 'If it doesn't, I don't know what we'll do.'

'We are going to do our best and try really hard.'

'Thanks, Alonzo, and good luck.'

Chapter 14

Where's Blaze?

Alonzo sets off across the fields towards William's house and notices that more things are the wrong way round. Now the sheep have big ears like elephants and the horses have webbed feet instead of hooves!

Goodness me, he thinks. It's a good job we're doing the plan today, because who knows how the world would end up!

As he arrives at William's house, the door bursts open and Alonzo gets dragged inside by William. 'It's today! It's today! We're going to sort out the world today!'

'William,' says Alonzo. 'You seem extraordinarily excited!'

'I am, Alonzo. What we are going to do is just amazing!'

'Well, yes it is, but we need to hope that my plan works.'

'Of course it will. If Alonzo the Magic Chicken can't sort this out, then nobody can.'

'I really hope so. Have you spoken with the other birds today? Are they full of confidence as well?'

'Yep, they're all good and raring to go. They can't wait!'

'Well, not long to wait now. Does everybody know what time to start?'

'Yep. All sorted.'

'Great. Let me show you what was delivered to me this morning.'

Alonzo shows William his headset microphone.

'That's so cool!' says William. 'I can't wait till 12 noon. It seems ages away.'

'I know, but it'll come round soon enough.'

'What time is Blaze coming round?'

'Any minute.'

They wait and wait but there's no sign of Blaze.

'What do you think has happened to him?' asks William. 'He said he would arrive early. It's nearly 11.30! The plan starts in 30 minutes!'

'Don't worry,' says Alonzo. 'I'm sure he's alright. Maybe he's busy.'

'Busy? Busy?! What on Earth can be more important than the plan? That Blaze is so full of himself sometimes...'

Suddenly, the door bursts open and Blaze tumbles through in a fluster of feathers. 'I am so sorry! I've had a dreadful morning. I overslept and only

woke up 10 minutes ago! With all the talk of different time zones, I confused myself and set my alarm clock for the wrong time! I had to fly super fast to get here,' he says breathlessly.

'My goodness. That is a bad start to the day,' says Alonzo. 'But you need to get your breath back quickly as the plan is due to start in 10 minutes. I need to get my headset on, and William, prepare yourself to fly with Blaze.'

Chapter 15

Go for Launch!

Alonzo tests his headset to make sure the Prime Minister can still hear him.

'Hi, Dave. Just to let you know that we're about to take off. This is the moment of truth. We'll keep flying until you tell us that things are getting back to normal.'

'OK. I'll keep you posted. Good luck!' replies the Prime Minister.

Alonzo walks outside and sees William sitting on Blaze's back, ready to flap with his one good wing. 'OK, you guys. This is it. Let's go!'

Blaze flaps his big, strong wings and soars into the sky. He looks back and sees Alonzo looking a little hesitant. 'Come on! You can do it! Just believe.'

Alonzo watches Blaze, takes a big gulp, flaps his little wings, and slowly but surely lifts off the ground. With each flap, he climbs higher and higher, until William's house is just a small dot.

As he looks around, he sees thousands of birds everywhere, all flying in the same direction, working together to create the necessary force to change the direction of the world. Wow, he thinks. This is awesome!

He soon spots some of his friends. There's Sara the Swan flying with elegance and ease; she makes it look so effortless. He then sees Nicola the Nightingale, who looks like she's struggling. As he flies over to her, her wings falter, stop moving and then she plummets towards the ground!

68

Before he can even react, Sara dips her wings and catches her. 'Thank you, Sara. My little wings are so tired already. Can I catch a ride on you for a little bit until I catch my breath? I'm not as fit as I thought.'

'Of course you can. Stay as long as you like, and jump off when you're ready.'

'Hello? Alonzo? How are you all doing up there?' says a voice in Alonzo's ear.

'Oh, hello, Dave. This is an amazing sight. There are thousands and thousands of birds up here. How are things looking with you?'

'Well, at the moment it is very, very windy and everything is still topsy-turvy.'

'We'll keep going. Let us know if you start to see anything change.'

'Will do,' replied the Prime Minister and hangs up.

Alonzo's wings are beginning to tire. 'Hey, Sara. Can I catch a ride?'

'Hop on. I know what hard work this can be, and I fly long distances regularly. I don't know how you are coping.'

'It is hard, but this is too important to give up now, and I think we're nearly there. The Prime Minister has told me it is very windy on Earth, so I'm hoping that we just need to fly a bit longer to have enough force to stop the world rotating and then to make it spin in the right direction.'

'Cool. Let's keep going,' replies Sara.

Chapter 16

All Birds Together

After what feels like several hours, Alonzo hears a very excited Prime Minister yelling in his ear. 'It's changing! It's changing! Alonzo, you're doing it! My dog has started to woof again! Keep going, you're nearly there!'

'Wahoo!' yells a delighted Alonzo. 'I need to pass the message on to all the birds that we've nearly done it. Keep me posted!'

Alonzo quickly tells Sara, who tells Nicola, who then passes the message on to Dr Darren Duck. 'Pass it on. Make sure everybody knows.'

Soon the whole sky is filled with the tweeting and chirping of excited birds. They know the plan is working and things

73

are almost back to normal. It won't be long now.

'How we doing, Dave? Is the sun yellow again?'

'Nearly. Half of it is still blue, but it is slowly changing. Should only be a matter of minutes now.'

'That's great news. As soon as it's completely changed, let me know, as I think that will mean that our mission has been accomplished.'

'Birds, keep going,' yells Alonzo. 'We've nearly done it. Just a couple more minutes and then everything will have changed back to normal.'

'It's changed! It's changed. We are all back to normal! Top banana!' shouts the Prime Minister 'I mean, yes, that really is a fantastic effort. Well done!'

'Sara! We've done it! Pass the message on. We can all stop flying now. The world is spinning the right way again.'

Alonzo realises he's exhausted. He can't wait to get back onto the ground and into William's house where he can rest. His wings ache so much. As he starts to slow down, he watches all the other birds slowly gliding back towards the ground, chattering with excitement. They should all feel very proud. What an achievement and absolutely everybody helped, he thinks.

'Hello, Alonzo? It's Dave. Thank you. I cannot tell you how grateful we all are. You are truly amazing. I know you must be tired now, but I would like to hold a little party for you and your friends tomorrow at 10 Downing Street. Say, 3pm?'

75

'That would be lovely, thank you. I'll let the birds know. Excuse me now, I need to go. I'll see you tomorrow.'

As Alonzo walks towards his friend's house, he is suddenly swept off his little feet by Blaze and William.

'We did it, and it's all down to you, Alonzo!' says William.

'Yes, we did,' Alonzo replies. 'I am so pleased everything has worked out for the best, but I really need to have a snooze. I am exhausted.'

'Of course, you must be after all that flying, as you're not used to it,' says Blaze sympathetically. 'Enjoy your sleep.'

'There's a spare bed in the little bedroom if you want to stay there instead of going home,' says William.

'That would be great, thank you,'

replies Alonzo as he walks to the room, drops onto the soft, snuggly bed and falls asleep.

Chapter 17

Party Plans

Finally, Alonzo wakes up, only to realise he has slept through the whole of yesterday afternoon, all last night, and it is now 8 o'clock the following morning!

My goodness me, I really was tired. I wonder how all the other birds are feeling, he thinks.

As he wanders into the lounge, Blaze and William are arguing. 'I think we should ask him,' says William.

'But what if he says no?' replies Blaze.

'Well, if he does, then it'll be for the right reasons. You know that Alonzo will know best.'

'What are you two wittering on about?'

Blaze and William look at each other and then back to Alonzo. 'You ask him,

because I'm not going to,' says Blaze.

'Alonzo,' says William. 'Last night we received a phone call from Cara the Chinstrap Penguin, saying that they had so much fun flying, they want to be able to do it all the time. So, can you cast a spell that will change all the non-flying birds into flying birds?'

Alonzo looks at his two friends with a serious look on his face. 'I'm afraid that's just not possible for two reasons. Firstly, my magic, as you know, William, is only for short-term things. And secondly, the non-flying birds, like myself, have to accept that they are not meant to fly. They are just as special as the birds who can fly. There is no point trying to be something that you're not.'

'Alonzo, you always know the right

thing to say. Blaze and I will pass that message on. Won't we, Blaze?'

'Yes, of course we will.'

'Just before you do that, I have been asked to attend a party at 3pm today in 10 Downing Street as a thank you for yesterday. I would obviously like you two to attend, but I thought we could ask some of the other birds as well. You know, Dr Darren Duck, Sara the Swan, Nicola the Nightingale, and any others that can get there. Would you please phone them for me?'

'It'll be our pleasure. Ooh, a party. I haven't been to one in ages!' says William. 'I'll put on a colourful sling to mark the occasion.'

'I'm off home now to get washed and changed ready for this afternoon.

I'll see you there,' calls Alonzo as he makes his way through the front door.

Chapter 18

Clucking Success

It's nearly 3pm and Alonzo is wearing his best hat and sunglasses, ready for the party.

As it's not too far to walk and it is a nice sunny day, with a yellow sun and bright blue sky, he sets off with a spring in his step.

It is so lovely to see everything the right way round again. Black and white cows, green grass and horses with hooves, he thinks. Thank goodness!

It doesn't take him long to reach 10 Downing Street, where he is welcomed by hoards of people waving flags and blowing horns.

I can't believe this is all for me! Alonzo thinks. People are holding out their hands

to shake his wings, and patting him on the back. At this rate, it will take me ages to actually get to the front door. But he stops to talk with every person who wants to speak to him.

Finally, he gets to the door, which is thrown wide open to reveal Prime Minister Dave Chaddlesworth. The crowd breaks out into a mass of whistling and clapping.

'Good afternoon, everyone,' says the Prime Minister. 'Please allow me to introduce Alonzo the Chicken. He is the one, with the help of his friends, who managed to get our planet back to how it should be, and turn the right way again. He is tremendous!'

'Oh, not really, Dave,' replies Alonzo, and as he looks around, he sees some of his friends sneaking out from the

inside of Number 10, with big smiles on their faces.

What do they know that I don't? he wonders, as Dave Chaddlesworth starts talking again.

'To celebrate this enormous achievement, it gives me great pleasure to award Alonzo a medal. This is the highest medal any chicken can receive. It is a Chicken of the British Empire, a CBE.'

The crowd erupts into a frenzy, and his friends are jumping up and down, hooting and whistling in delight.

'Honestly, Prime Minister, I didn't expect this at all. I don't really feel I deserve this.'

'Let me be the judge of that. I think you do. So do all these other people and your friends. Stand tall, be proud. Ladies

and Gentleman, I give you Alonzo the Chicken CBE. He never let his feathers get ruffled and didn't chicken out once. He really has done us all a good turn!'

As the laughter and applause die down, Alonzo looks towards all his friends, gives them a big grin and a thumbs up. 'We did it!' he says triumphantly.

The End

Spot the Difference

See if you can find all 10 differences between these two very similar pictures.

Having trouble? Then contact the author for help at www.facebook.com/alonzothechicken

Acknowledgements

Firstly I would like to thank the very talented Monika Filipina Trzpil, who completely brings my characters to life with her amazing illustrations.

Then a big thank you to all my family and friends who have supported me, especially those who have allowed me to use their good names in my story.

Thanks also to Dave Chapman, who read the story and came up with some 'cracking' ideas which I have shamelessly used.

Lastly, to all those who believed in a little, superhero chicken called Alonzo; I thank you.

Debbie Kelly 2013

About the Author

Debbie is the author of Alonzo and Molly
the Mermaid, the first book in the Alonzo
the Chicken series, published in 2012.

When not dreaming up poultry adventures,
Debbie enjoys jive dancing, static trapeze,
skiing and spending quality time with her friends
and family. She currently lives in Newbury,
England with her rescue cat, Bella.

Look out for more great adventures
in the Alonzo series.

Alonzo and Molly the Mermaid
Alonzo and the All-Eyed Monster
Alonzo and the Gummy Shark

You can keep up to date on all things Alonzo
online on Facebook: alonzothechicken. If you have
any questions, email the author, Debbie Kelly,
at debbie@alonzothechicken.com

'Alonzo and the Meteorite' is also available to
read in new-fangled, digital format for your iPad
or ebook reader. To download it search for 'Alonzo
The Chicken' on the iBookstore or Kindle store.

Visit www.digitalleaf.co.uk
for more stories and apps

facebook: digitalleafuk twitter: digitalleafuk